# A Robbie Reader

# Tsunami Disaster in Indonesia, 2004

John Torres

## Mitchell Lane
## PUBLISHERS

P.O. Box 196
Hockessin, Delaware 19707
Visit us on the web: www.mitchelllane.com
Comments? email us: mitchelllane@mitchelllane.com

Printing          2          3          4          5          6          7          8          9

**A Robbie Reader/Natural Disasters**

Library of Congress Cataloging-in-Publication Data
Torres, John Albert.
    Tsunami Disaster in Indonesia, 2004 / by John Torres.
        p. cm. — (Natural disasters—what can we learn?)
    Includes bibliographical references and index.
    ISBN 1-58415-415-2 (lib. bd.)
    1. Indian Ocean Tsunami, 2004—Juvenile literature.  2. Tsunamis—Indian Ocean—
Juvenile literature.  I. Title.  II. Series.
    GC221.5.T67 2005
    959.804—dc22
                                                                                                2005004248

ISBN-10: 1-58415-415-2                                    ISBN-13: 978-1-58415-415-0

**ABOUT THE AUTHOR: John A. Torres** is an award-winning journalist who covers social issues for *Florida Today*. John has also written more than 25 books for various publishers on a variety of topics. He wrote *P. Diddy, Clay Aiken, Mia Hamm,* and *Fitness Stars of Bodybuilding* for Mitchell Lane Publishers. In his spare time John likes playing sports, going to theme parks, and fishing with his children, stepchildren and wife, Jennifer.

**PHOTO CREDITS:** Cover John Torres; pp. 4, 6 John Torres; pp. 8, 10 Getty Images; p. 12 Andrea Pickens; pp. 14, 15, 16, 18, 20, 22, 24, 25, 26, 27 John Torres.

**PUBLISHER'S NOTE:** This story is based on the author's extensive research, including his personal trip to Indonesia in January 2005, where he witnessed the devastation firsthand and spoke to dozens of survivors.

The internet sites referenced herein were active as of the publication date. Due to the fleeting nature of some websites, we cannot guarantee they will be active when you are reading this book.

# TABLE OF CONTENTS

Words in **bold** type can be found in the glossary.

Many mothers in Indonesia lost children to the tsunami. This woman lost nearly 40 members of her family.

# THE BABY IS GONE

Wong Li Khiun was a young Chinese mother living in Banda Aceh (BON-dah ah-CHAY), **Indonesia** (in-doe-NEE-zha). She loved her husband and her three-year-old son very much. The family lived near a beach on the Indian Ocean. It was one of the most beautiful places in the world. Her life was perfect.

Then something terrible happened.

On the morning of December 26, 2004, a powerful **earthquake** (URTH-kwake) rumbled along the ocean floor. Wong Li ran outside with her son. They prayed until the terrible shaking stopped.

#### CHAPTER ONE

This house was the only one left standing near the coast in Meulaboh, Indonesia.

It finally did, and they went back inside the house. A few minutes later, there was a knock at their front door. They heard the screams of people running by their house. The earthquake had caused a **tsunami** (soo-NAH-mee), or a series of giant waves. The waves were traveling at the speed of a jet plane. The water was coming up out of the ocean and into the city.

Wong Li's husband told her to take their son and run. Then he hurried away to help his parents get out of their house. The water was already up to Wong Li's waist. Suddenly a strong wave came. She and her son were swept farther down the road. She couldn't stand. Somehow she was able to grab a utility pole. Her son held on to her tightly.

More and more people came to the pole. It was their only chance of living. But there were too many people. They knocked Wong Li off the pole into the rushing water. Her son fell off and was swept away. Wong Li screamed.

"I saw him go under five times," Wong Li cried a few weeks later when she spoke with the author of this book. "Then he called for me and went under for the last time."

Wong Li thought she would drown too. Somehow she was able to live. When the water went back into the ocean, she found her husband.

"Where is the baby?" he asked her.

"The baby is gone."

As a tsunami wave crashes ashore, some people flee, but others stand and watch.

# WHAT IS A TSUNAMI?

*Tsunami* is a Japanese word that means "harbor wave." Tsunamis can happen when there are undersea earthquakes or when volcanoes (vahl-KAY-nose) erupt. A tsunami can also take place if a giant **meteor** (MEE-tee-or) crashes into the ocean.

An undersea earthquake makes the ocean floor rise up and then fall back down. When that happens, the water forms giant waves. The waves travel away from the earthquake in opposite directions. When they are in deep water, tsunami waves are not very high. But they are long and travel very fast. A tsunami can be more than 100 miles long and move at

500 miles per hour! Ocean water rises and falls in **cycles** (SY-kuls) we call tides. The tides are controlled by the magnetic pull of the moon.

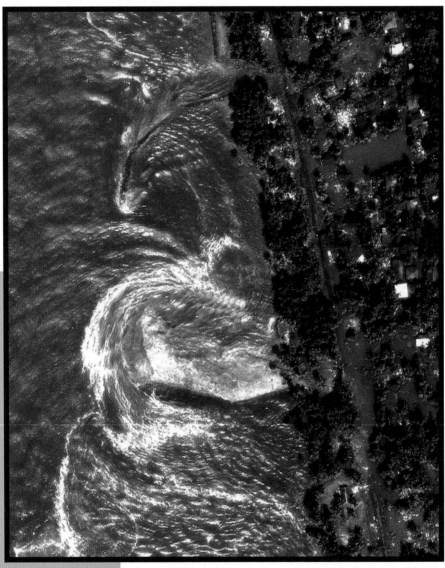

This satellite photo, taken on December 26, 2004, shows the coastline of Kalutara, Sri Lanka, after it has been hit by a tsunami wave.

A tsunami is like a high tide that doesn't stop rising. When it reaches the beach, it forms a wall of water. Sometimes a tsunami can be 100 feet high. It destroys anything in its path— even houses, buildings, and cars.

The Indian Ocean tsunami of December 26, 2004, formed because an underwater earthquake happened 100 miles off the western coast of Sumatra (soo-MAH-tra). Wong Li lives on Sumatra. It is one of the large islands that make up the country of Indonesia.

A few minutes after the earthquake, the water rose and the tsunami changed the world forever. Nature can be very strange. One minute it can be a calm, beautiful day and another minute there can be a terrible storm. It is also strange how animals and birds seem to know what is going to happen. Moments before the water rose up onto the land, crabs came scurrying out of the water. Monkeys, tigers, and elephants all ran to higher ground away from the ocean. More than 200,000 people died in the Indian Ocean disaster, but the animals lived.

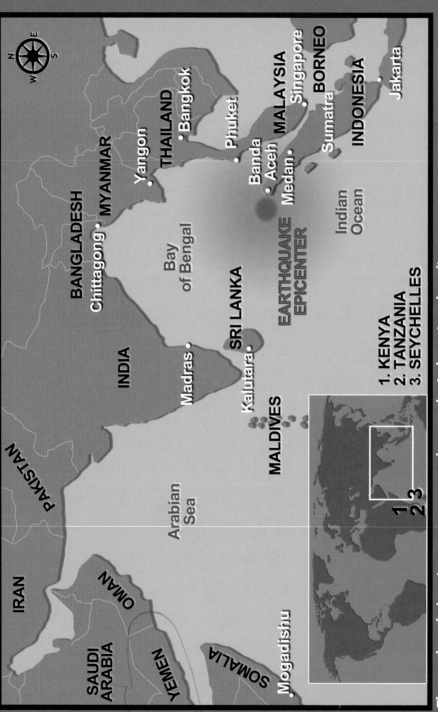

The earthquake's epicenter was very close to the Indonesian shoreline.

# THE SCOPE OF THE DISASTER

Even though the earthquake happened very close to Indonesia, the tsunami was so big and powerful that it crashed into many countries. The waves traveled the entire distance of the Indian Ocean. Besides Indonesia, the tsunami killed people in Sri Lanka (sree LAHNG-kah), India, Thailand (TIE-land), Somalia (so-MAH-lee-ah), Maldives (MALL-deevs), Malaysia (muh-LAY-zheh), Myanmar (MY-an-MAR), Bangladesh (bahn-gleh-DESH), Tanzania (tan-zan-EE-uh), Kenya, and Seychelles (say-SHELL). The tsunami was so powerful that scientists said it even raised water a little bit in New Jersey and Florida!

Throughout coastal areas of Sumatra are piles of debris where houses used to stand.

The countries of Southeast Asia (AY-jha) were **devastated** (DEV-uh-stay-ted). In Thailand, more than 12,000 children died. Entire villages in India were destroyed. Indonesia suffered the most. More than 100,000 people died in the two cities of Banda Aceh and Meulaboh (MOO-la-boe). People spent days and weeks looking for their lost children. They tried to clear away the rubble that used to be their homes.

At a refugee center, a woman and her son look at posters of people missing in the tsunami.

Every single house along the beach was crushed. There were dead bodies everywhere. Boats had been hurled onto the land and were found next to cars that had been flipped upside down.

People searched and searched for family members. Zuli Nuzuli spent weeks looking for his 18-year-old daughter. She had been swept away by a wave.

The reflection of a destroyed house can be seen in the water left behind by the tsunami.

The town of Meulaboh lay in ruins.

"I will keep looking for her," he told the author as tears rolled down his face.

There were people like Zulfahmi Tarmizi, a 10-year-old boy who lost his parents and his brothers and sisters. At least his grandmother was alive. He hugged her tight when he saw her. She would take care of him.

Nobody really knew what to do. There were no homes for them to return to. There were no jobs to work. There were no schools for children to attend. There was no food to eat or clean water to drink. Parents were left without children and children were left without parents. The people were **suffering** (SUH-fur-ing). They needed help with everything. It was time for the world to respond. But would enough people be willing to help?

Graffiti marks the date of the killer tsunami, December 26, 2004.

Refugees in Medan are being evacuated to other areas.

# THE WORLD CRIES, THEN HELPS

When news of the killer tsunami spread to the rest of the world, people everywhere were stunned. It was one of the worst natural disasters in history.

A few days after the tsunami caused the Indian Ocean to rise up onto the land, experts and government officials said that hundreds of thousands of people could be dead. This news made people around the world very sad.

It also made them want to help. Everywhere, people wanted to get involved, from little children bringing money to school for a special collection to organizations (org-in-uh-ZAY-shuns) like Red Cross International (in-tur-NA-shun-uhl) and the United Nations.

#### CHAPTER FOUR

Indonesian soldiers load food onto a French cargo plane for the tsunami victims.

Governments around the world reacted quickly. They promised to send billions of dollars worth of aid for food, water, and medicine. They also sent soldiers and ships, planes, and helicopters. U.S. President George W. Bush sent the aircraft carrier *Abraham Lincoln* and more than 20 other U.S. Navy ships to Indonesia to help the people.

In a disaster like this, there is not enough food for people to eat, and the water gets dirty. People can get very sick and die if they drink dirty water. Countries like Australia and Spain sent over big machines to help make the water clean.

Soldiers worked hard to clear the roads so that supply trucks could arrive. Others looked for dead bodies and helped put homeless people into **refugee** (REF-you-JEE) centers, where they could sleep and get food and see doctors.

Many doctors, nurses, and relief workers volunteered to go to the disaster sites and help out. The people in some of these countries, like Indonesia, were not used to having so many **foreign** (FOR-un) people in their country.

But they were happy. The world had come to help.

A man poses with his rickshaw in front of tsunami debris.

# YEARS OF REBUILDING

Weeks after the tsunami killed so many people and destroyed so many other lives, there was finally a glimmer of hope. No major diseases, like **malaria** (muh-LAIR-ee-uh) or **cholera** (KAH-luh-ruh), had cropped up. Help was making it to people in need. The world was following through on the promises it had made.

There was talk of making the damaged areas even better and nicer than they had been before. But there would be years of rebuilding ahead. It would also take years for some people to recover. It is hard to go on when you've lost everything you had.

Maybe the most important result was a plan to create a warning system for the Indian

Donations of rice, eggs, and vegetables have made it to a refugee camp in Sumatra.

Ocean. With a tsunami warning system, people probably would have had time to escape from their houses and run to higher, safer ground. Thousands of lives could have been saved. The United States has a warning system located in the Pacific Ocean. It was too far away to provide warnings to people in the Indian Ocean.

The December 26 tsunami was a terrible disaster, one of the worst of all time. Hundreds of thousands of people were killed and millions

Despite the tragedy, Indonesian children are eager to get on with their lives.

of homes were destroyed. But one thing that happened because of the tsunami was that new friendships between people and governments were formed. For example, the United States and Indonesia were never really friends with each other. Now the two countries are working closely together and becoming friends. Also, people are learning about other parts of the world and respecting how other people live.

Maybe those feelings of helping each other will continue even after people recover from the tsunami.

Jakarta, the capital of Indonesia, received little tsunami damage.

The main road in Meulaboh is awash in mud left behind by the killer wave.

Two U.S. Navy ships assist in relief efforts.

Two children in Medan, Indonesia, walk home together after school.

Relief volunteers assemble boxes of supplies.

Indonesian children smile at a news camera.

# CHRONOLOGY

| | |
|---|---|
| **Dec. 25, 2004** | Christmas is celebrated in many places around the world. |
| **Dec. 26, 2004** | An earthquake off the coast of Sumatra rips the ocean floor shortly before 8:00 A.M., forming a tsunami. |
| | Fifteen minutes later the tsunami engulfs Banda Aceh in Indonesia. |
| | Seven hours after the earthquake, the tsunami kills people and damages property on the coast of Africa. |
| **Dec. 30, 2004** | Tsunami death toll reaches 118,000. |
| **Dec. 31, 2004** | The United States promises $350 million in aid. |
| **Jan. 1, 2005** | USS *Abraham Lincoln* arrives off the coast of Sumatra, bringing supplies and people to help out. |
| **Jan. 3, 2005** | Japan promises $500 million in aid. |
| **Jan. 5, 2005** | Australia promises $800 million in aid. |
| **Jan. 19, 2005** | Tsunami death toll soars past 212,000. |
| **Sept. 26, 2005** | Indonesia's President Susilo Bambang Yudhoyono urges the world to honor its pledges; only one third of the promised aid has arrived. |

# OTHER MAJOR TSUNAMIS

**1755**   An earthquake, causing a tsunami and fires, kills an estimated 60,000 people in Lisbon, Portugal.

**1883**   A volcanic eruption near Krakatau, Indonesia, creates a tsunami that kills more than 36,000 people.

**1896**   A 100-foot-high tsunami in Japan causes 27,000 deaths.

**1923**   A Japanese tsunami kills 130,000 people.

**1929**   A very rare Atlantic Ocean tsunami strikes the Canadian province of Newfoundland, killing about 30 people.

**1946**   A tsunami strikes Hilo, Hawaii, and kills about 160 people.

**1952**   A tsunami that begins off the east coast of Russia causes extensive property damage but very few deaths.

**1960**   The most powerful earthquake in the 20th century, off the coast of Chile, generates a tsunami that kills about 3,000 people in Chile, Hawaii, and Japan.

**1964**   An earthquake in Alaska generates a tsunami that hits Washington, Oregon, and California; more than 100 people lose their lives.

**1998**   Three tsunamis strike Papua, New Guinea, killing 2,000 people.

# FIND OUT MORE

## Books

Bonar, Samantha. *Tsunamis.* Mankato, Minnesota: Capstone Press, 2001.

Drohan, Michele Ingber. *Tsunamis: Killer Waves.* New York: Powerkids Press, 1999.

Jennings, Terry. *Floods and Tidal Waves.* North Mankato, Minnesota: Thameside Press, 2000.

Souza, Dorothy M. *Powerful Waves.* Minneapolis, Minnesota: Carolrhoda Books, 1992.

Steele, Christy. *Tsunamis.* Chicago: Raintree, 2001.

## On the Internet

FEMA for Kids: Tsunami
http://www.fema.gov/kids/tsunami.htm

National Geographic Kids: Killer Wave! Tsunami
http://www.nationalgeographic.com/ngkids/9610/kwave/

Tsunami—Enchanted Learning
http://www.enchantedlearning.com/subjects/tsunami/

# GLOSSARY

**cholera** (KAH-luh-ruh)—a serious form of diarrhea that is often deadly.

**cycles** (SY-kuls)—the rising and falling of ocean water.

**devastated** (DEV-uh-stay-ted)—totally destroyed.

**earthquake** (URTH-kwake)—shaking and vibration at the surface of the earth resulting from underground movement.

**foreign** (FOR-un)—born in or belonging to a country different from the one you are in.

**Indonesia** (in-doe-NEE-zha)—a country in Southeast Asia consisting of many islands.

**malaria** (muh-LAIR-ee-uh)—a disease with alternating chills and fever; spread by mosquitoes.

**meteor** (MEE-tee-or)—a particle from space that enters the earth's atmosphere.

**refugee** (REF-you-JEE)—a person who leaves an area to escape danger.

**suffering** (SUH-fur-ing)—living in pain and sadness.

**tsunami** (soo-NAH-mee)—a series of giant waves.

# INDEX